Samuel French Acting Edition

Nylon

by Sofia Alvarez

FOR PRODUCTION ENQUIRIES

UNITED STATES AND CANADA
info@concordtheatricals.com
1-866-979-0447

UNITED KINGDOM AND EUROPE
licensing@concordtheatricals.co.uk
020-7054-7200

Each title is subject to availability from Concord Theatricals, depending upon country of performance. Please be aware that *NYLON* may not be licensed by Concord Theatricals in your territory. Professional and amateur producers should contact the nearest Concord Theatricals office or licensing partner to verify availability.

For all enquiries regarding motion picture, television, and other media rights, please contact Concord Theatricals.

MUSIC USE NOTE

Licensees are solely responsible for obtaining formal written permission from copyright owners to use copyrighted music in the performance of this play and are strongly cautioned to do so. If no such permission is obtained by the licensee, then the licensee must use only original music that the licensee owns and controls. Licensees are solely responsible and liable for all music clearances and shall indemnify the copyright owners of the play(s) and their licensing agent, Concord Theatricals, against any costs, expenses, losses and liabilities arising from the use of music by licensees. Please contact the appropriate music licensing authority in your territory for the rights to any incidental music.

IMPORTANT BILLING AND CREDIT REQUIREMENTS

If you have obtained performance rights to this title, please refer to your licensing agreement for important billing and credit requirements.

NYLON was first produced by Nicola Korzenko for Blockchain Theater Project (BTP) at Theaterlab in New York City in March of 2019. The performance was directed by Knud Adams, with sets by Andrew Moerdyk, costumes by Clara Fath, lighting design by Kate McGee, sound design by John Gasper, and original music by Anand Wilder. The production stage manager was Pat Harnett-Marshall. The cast was as follows:

ANNA . . . . Sheila Vand

MATTHEW . . . . Cesar J. Rosado

MARISOL . . . . Maggie Bofill

GIGI . . . . Claire Siebers

COLIN . . . . Brian Miskell

CHARACTERS

ANNA – (early thirties) A magazine editor living in London. American.

MATTHEW – (early thirties) Anna's ex-boyfriend. A rooftop gardener and former musician living in New York. American.

MARISOL – (fifties) The mother of Matthew's former bandmate. A homemaker living in Princeton, New Jersey. American.

GIGI – (mid-twenties) Matthew's girlfriend. A waitress living in New York. American.

COLIN – (mid- to late thirties) Anna's husband. A civil servant living in London. English.

SETTING

The play takes place back and forth between New York, London, and Princeton, New Jersey. The locations are as follows:

ACT ONE

– An East Village coffee shop with a nineties vibe – not because it's hipped out in a 2010s way, but because it has not been renovated since the nineties.

– A subway platform.

– A mid-range hotel room in Midtown.

ACT TWO

– The living room of Marisol's house in Princeton, New Jersey. It's tasteful, if a little antiquated and formal.

– Two cafés in New York City. They may be the same coffee shop from the first act, or new locations.

– Anna and Colin's flat in London. Stylish in a boring, sterile way.

TIME

The 2010s

AUTHOR'S NOTE

In the first production of *Nylon*, both Matthew and Marisol were played by Hispanic actors. This was intentional but is not a necessity. Should you choose not to cast the play this way, please change the dialogue that is currently in Spanish back to the English option listed in brackets.

All characters may be played by actors of any ethnicity so long as the casting makes sense for the questions the play raises surrounding who is related to whom.

ACT I

1.1 New York

(**ANNA** *and* **MATTHEW** *sit in a coffee shop in the East Village.*)

ANNA. It's nice to see you.

MATTHEW. Yeah. You too.

ANNA. Strange. How long.

MATTHEW. Mm-hm.

ANNA. That it's happening now.

MATTHEW. Well, yeah. You sent me all those e-mails.

ANNA. Because you didn't respond to me at first.

MATTHEW. I thought maybe if I ignored you.

ANNA. Are you being serious?

MATTHEW. No, I'm kidding.

ANNA. But it did take you a few weeks to respond.

MATTHEW. I was just surprised, that's all.

ANNA. Yeah.

(*Small beat.*)

MATTHEW. We didn't have to meet in this neighborhood you know.

ANNA. I know. I thought it would be convenient for you.

MATTHEW. Well, sure, but I mean – I would've come to you.

ANNA. I'm in Midtown – a hotel near the conference. You hate it up there.

MATTHEW. I'm just saying – I would've done it.

ANNA. Where would we have gone up there, Starbucks?

MATTHEW. What's the difference?

ANNA. Anyway it's fine. It's nice to get out of Midtown.

MATTHEW. So. How are you?

ANNA. I'm good. You?

MATTHEW. Good.

ANNA. You ordered a tea.

MATTHEW. Yeah.

ANNA. Are you off caffeine or something?

MATTHEW. No.

ANNA. Oh. I was just wondering. You were always such a coffee guy.

MATTHEW. I like tea.

ANNA. Cool. Me too.

MATTHEW. How's your conference?

ANNA. It's good.

MATTHEW. Really?

ANNA. It's, you know – boring but necessary.

MATTHEW. Yeah?

ANNA. Completely unnecessary but required.

MATTHEW. Got it.

ANNA. And you?

MATTHEW. What about me?

ANNA. How's work?

MATTHEW. It's great.

MATTHEW.	**ANNA.**
So how long are you in town?	What's going on with –

ANNA. Sorry, what?

MATTHEW. How long are you here?

ANNA. 'Til Tuesday.

MATTHEW. Oh, that sucks.

ANNA. What?

MATTHEW. That you have to stay through the weekend.

ANNA. Oh.

MATTHEW. I'm sure you'd like to be home is all.

ANNA. Right.

MATTHEW. How's your family?

ANNA. They're good.

MATTHEW. Your parents still in Seattle?

ANNA. Yep. How's your mom?

MATTHEW. Good – loves being a grandmother as I'm sure you can imagine.

ANNA. Grandmother?

MATTHEW. Oh, Gerard had a baby.

ANNA. He did?

MATTHEW. Yeah – sorry I thought you – /

ANNA. With – /

MATTHEW. Caroline.

ANNA. Whoa.

MATTHEW. I would've – I just thought you already – /

ANNA. No. I didn't know.

MATTHEW. Oh, well – yeah – there's that.

ANNA. So how old is your... / nephew?

MATTHEW. Nephew, yeah, he's two and a half.

ANNA. Wow. Old.

MATTHEW. So yeah – pretty soon after –

ANNA. I guess I just missed it.

MATTHEW. How's your sister?

ANNA. She's good.

MATTHEW. Still in San Francisco?

ANNA. Yep.

MATTHEW. Married?

ANNA. Engaged.

MATTHEW. To Henry?

ANNA. Nope – new guy.

MATTHEW. And she's engaged? That's fast.

ANNA. Not really. They've been together awhile.

MATTHEW. Is she still making jewelry?

ANNA. She's in law school.

MATTHEW. Oh. Weird. Do you think she'll be a lawyer?

ANNA. That's typically why people go to law school.

MATTHEW. I didn't mean anything by it – /

ANNA. I know.

(Beat. **MATTHEW** *looks around.)*

MATTHEW. Man, this place sucks, huh?

ANNA. You picked it.

MATTHEW. I know but don't you kind of feel like it sucks –
do these people realize they all look like they're wearing
costumes?

ANNA. Yeah, okay – it totally sucks.

(They both smile.)

MATTHEW. Do you get back here much?

ANNA. Occasionally. For work or, you know. We spent some
time here last year.

MATTHEW. Oh right, I think I knew that. Jo or somebody
mentioned it.

ANNA. Do you still talk to Jo?

MATTHEW. A bit. Not really. You?

ANNA. Not so much. We used to keep in touch more, when
I first moved.

MATTHEW. People aren't really around.

ANNA. Nobody?

MATTHEW. Nah. Things aren't like how they were. No one
hangs out.

ANNA. Yeah, that was starting to happen even before I left.

MATTHEW. Well, things sort of fell apart after the funeral if
we want to be blunt about it.

ANNA. Right, of course, but even before that, there was
kind of a shift.

MATTHEW. Sure.

(Beat.)

(ANNA looks around.)

(Maybe she taps her finger on her coffee cup and her wedding ring clinks against it.)

(Or, MATTHEW just happens to look at her left hand.)

(Or, it's just that point in the conversation.)

MATTHEW. And how is he?

ANNA. Colin? He's fine.

MATTHEW. What's he doing tonight?

ANNA. I don't know – maybe at the pub with some friends.

MATTHEW. Is that his thing – the pub with some friends.

ANNA. Don't make fun of him.

MATTHEW. I'm making fun of you.

ANNA. For what?

MATTHEW. You're in New York – call it a bar.

ANNA. Well, over there – where he is – it's called a pub so give me a break, okay?

MATTHEW. Hey, Anna, I'm not trying to pick a fight with you.

ANNA. Okay then don't pick a fight with me.

(Slight pause.)

You still haven't said what you're doing for work.

MATTHEW. I'm not playing music if that's what you're getting at.

ANNA. I mean I guess I sort of knew that.

MATTHEW. You're checking up on me?

ANNA. No, I just mean I haven't seen anything new. Online or whatever.

(Small beat.)

So what are you doing?

MATTHEW. I'm gardening.

ANNA. Excuse me?

MATTHEW. Gardening.

ANNA. Like in parks?

MATTHEW. I have a partner who I convert space with, mainly people's roofs, we build some boxes, plant flowers or tomatoes or herbs or something and then I tend to the space weekly or bi-weekly or whatever until the owners can handle it themselves.

ANNA. Wow.

MATTHEW. Yeah. It's good, lucrative, sustainable rooftop gardening. And I like it.

ANNA. That's great.

MATTHEW. It is. This is something that I'm happy about.

ANNA. Then I'm happy for you.

MATTHEW. Thanks.

ANNA. How did you start? Gardening.

MATTHEW. It just sort of happened.

ANNA. But come on, you're still playing, right, like recording your own stuff?

MATTHEW. No, I'm not recording music. I don't play anymore. Even on the side.

ANNA. So you gave up?

MATTHEW. I didn't give up. I'm taking a break I guess.

ANNA. What does that mean?

MATTHEW. I don't want to have this conversation with you.

ANNA. Why not?

MATTHEW. Because I don't want to leave here feeling like shit with my balls in your purse.

ANNA. I'm not trying to upset you. I'm trying to understand.

MATTHEW. Don't get me started, okay? You're a magazine editor, you're not exactly changing the world.

ANNA. I like my job.

MATTHEW. Your job is fluff. People throw your job away. There are used tampons in trash cans on your job.

ANNA. Fine. I understand, degrade me to avoid talking about yourself.

MATTHEW. I like gardening. I'm good at it. Bitchy women you would be friends with hire me. They did a piece on me in New York Magazine.

ANNA. What an accomplishment. How many used tampons are sitting on top of that in someone's trash right now?

(*Pause.*)

MATTHEW. Anna...

ANNA. I don't want to fight with you.

MATTHEW. Me neither. I'm sorry.

ANNA. Me too.

(*A pause. She looks around.*)

I like it here.

MATTHEW. In this shitty coffee shop?

ANNA. No, in New York. I miss it.

MATTHEW. You should come back.

ANNA. It's not that easy. But it is nice to see you.

MATTHEW. Yeah. It's nice to see you too.

ANNA. And you're good?

MATTHEW. I am. I like my job. And I don't miss music. So please don't give me a hard time about it, okay?

ANNA. Okay.

(*Beat.*)

MATTHEW. Are you hungry?

ANNA. Yes. I'm hungry.

MATTHEW. Well we could have a day-old pastry here or go somewhere.

ANNA. You think that's a good idea?

MATTHEW. Why not?

ANNA. It's dinnertime – I don't know, I wasn't suggesting, a meal, I –

MATTHEW. Right. I forgot, you're crazy.

(*He smiles.*)

ANNA. I'm sorry.

MATTHEW. It's okay.

ANNA. How about –

MATTHEW. Yeah?

ANNA. Maybe we could – order something.

MATTHEW. Order?

ANNA. You know, like, something inside. I don't think I can go to a restaurant with you it just – it feels too *planned*.

MATTHEW. So you can plan to get together with me but you can't plan to have dinner with me?

(**ANNA** *shrugs.*)

You want to come to my apartment?

ANNA. No. God no. That sounds horrible.

MATTHEW. Your hotel?

ANNA. I don't want to give you the wrong idea.

MATTHEW. Of course not.

ANNA. Room service dinner, then you go home.

MATTHEW. I wouldn't stay.

ANNA. I was telling myself, not you. I know you wouldn't stay.

MATTHEW. Sure.

ANNA. Really?

MATTHEW. If that's what you want –

ANNA. I'm sorry if this is weird. I just feel like we haven't even really talked yet, you know?

MATTHEW. No, let's hang out. We'll go to your hotel.

ANNA. Restaurants – just, too much noise, too many people. Or not enough people – and that's even worse.

MATTHEW. I get it. You don't have to keep explaining yourself. And I want to keep hanging out with you. So yeah, let's go to your hotel.

ANNA. Okay, great.

1.2 Later

*(**ANNA** and **MATTHEW** stand on a subway platform. **ANNA** talks quickly, nervously.)*

ANNA. ...And I thought I wouldn't like the new EIC but it's been actually kind of great because it's made me realize –

(She stops talking as a loud train passes.)

...That whereas I thought the old editor really liked me and had my back she was actually very competitive with me and dismissive of my ideas – whereas the new EIC is more direct and will say outright when she doesn't like something but when she does like my work is very complimentary so I know that she actually means it.

*(**MATTHEW** picks up the collar of **ANNA**'s coat and pulls it more closely around her.)*

MATTHEW. You look cold.

ANNA. Oh, I'm not.

MATTHEW. And skinny.

ANNA. Excuse me?

MATTHEW. I couldn't stop thinking at the coffee shop – "She looks too skinny."

ANNA. That's what you were thinking?

MATTHEW. Yeah.

ANNA. You look buff. All that gardening.

MATTHEW. Let's call it landscaping.

ANNA. But its not, is it?

MATTHEW. Kind of.

ANNA. Man this train, huh?

MATTHEW. You're the one who didn't want to take a cab.

ANNA. I know. The image of it just seemed wrong.

MATTHEW. Of us in a cab?

ANNA. Doesn't it?

MATTHEW. You're insane.

ANNA. I know.

MATTHEW. I know you know.

>   *(Beat.)*

I'm glad you're happy at work.

ANNA. Thanks.

MATTHEW. New editor sounds good.

ANNA. She is.

MATTHEW. You need a straight shooter. You don't do well with competition.

ANNA. I was doing well before.

MATTHEW. That wasn't a dig. I'm not trying to fight with you.

ANNA. Right, I know. Sorry. I'm glad you're happy at work too.

MATTHEW. You don't mean that.

ANNA. I'm trying to be positive.

MATTHEW. I know, I appreciate it.

ANNA. And I promise not to ask you about music again.

MATTHEW. Good.

ANNA. If we can talk about – other stuff.

MATTHEW. What other stuff?

ANNA. Not here, later.

MATTHEW. Okay.

>   *(Longish pause.)*

ANNA. Hey.

MATTHEW. Yeah?

>   *(Small beat.)*

ANNA. Twelve.

>   *(Beat. He looks at her. Then:)*

MATTHEW. Female.

>   *(Another beat.)*

ANNA. Nine?

MATTHEW. Male. We know that nine is male. You're giving me easy ones.

ANNA. Twenty-one?

MATTHEW. Male, again.

>*(Small beat.)*

Eleven.

ANNA. I think eleven is a transwoman.

MATTHEW. Can numbers be trans?

ANNA. They can if they can be gendered.

MATTHEW. Fair enough.

ANNA. Nineteen?

MATTHEW. Male. Fifty-six?

ANNA. Female.

>*(Beat. She looks at him.)*

Four.

MATTHEW. We know this one.

ANNA. But they're allowed to change.

MATTHEW. I still think male.

ANNA. Really?

MATTHEW. You think female?

ANNA. No I guess you're right. Four is still male.

>*(Beat.)*

MATTHEW. Thirty-two?

ANNA. I don't want to play anymore. It's silly.

>*(Beat. They look around.)*

MATTHEW. I ran into your friend Nat a few weeks ago.

ANNA. Really, where?

MATTHEW. Just, like, on the street.

ANNA. How is she?

MATTHEW. She seemed good. She told me she misses you.

ANNA. People seem to.

MATTHEW. Don't be that way.

ANNA. What way?

MATTHEW. Sarcastic.

ANNA. I'm sorry but whenever I talk to someone from the States they always say that people miss me but it's just something to say. No one actually misses me.

MATTHEW. How do you know?

ANNA. Because it's true. No one ever calls me, no one ever comes to visit.

MATTHEW. Everyone is wrapped up in their own lives, I wouldn't take it personally.

ANNA. Exactly – everyone is wrapped up and I am too. Only with me they can blame me for it because I'm the one that moved – it's ridiculous.

MATTHEW. No one's blaming you.

ANNA. Yes – yes they are. They're all blaming me for not marrying you.

MATTHEW. Who is they? There's no they.

ANNA. I don't know. People.

MATTHEW. I don't blame you.

ANNA. No, not you. You should be thanking me.

MATTHEW. Anna, what are you doing?

ANNA. Don't make me feel like I'm crazy, okay?

MATTHEW. I'm not doing anything.

ANNA. I'm really happy, Matthew.

MATTHEW. I know.

ANNA. So don't think the reason I wanted to see you was because I'm not.

MATTHEW. I don't.

ANNA. I have a really nice life.

MATTHEW. I know you do.

ANNA. Colin makes me happy.

MATTHEW. I know.

ANNA. I just wanted to say it.

MATTHEW. And now you have.

ANNA. Yeah.

MATTHEW. So you can relax.

ANNA. Yeah.

MATTHEW. Great.

>*(Beat.)*

Here comes the train.

1.3 Later

(They enter Anna's hotel room.)

MATTHEW. Pretty normal, huh?

ANNA. What?

MATTHEW. Well it's not exactly like in the movies is it?

ANNA. Magazine editing? No – it's not.

MATTHEW. Still nice though.

ANNA. I don't have to pay for it – that's good enough for me.

MATTHEW. Do you have a per diem?

ANNA. Of course.

MATTHEW. So can we take something out of the minibar?

ANNA. I'm not drinking with you.

MATTHEW. Why not?

ANNA. Because it's a bad idea.

MATTHEW. You and these rules.

ANNA. How about dinner?

MATTHEW. Dinner sounds good.

ANNA. What do you want?

MATTHEW. Whatever.

ANNA. Burger?

MATTHEW. Sure.

ANNA. Fries?

MATTHEW. Salad.

ANNA. We'll get one of each and share.

MATTHEW. Okay.

*(**ANNA** picks up the phone.)*

ANNA. Hi. I'm in Room 604. I'd like to order. Yeah. Two cheeseburgers. Medium. Swiss. One with fries, one salad. Great. Thanks.

(She hangs up.)

MATTHEW. You do that so efficiently.

ANNA. So?

MATTHEW. I admire it.

ANNA. The way I talk to the room service guy?

MATTHEW. Yeah.

ANNA. That's weird.

MATTHEW. I was trying to compliment you.

ANNA. Thanks.

>   *(Beat.)*

MATTHEW. What are we gonna do while we wait for the food if we're not allowed to drink?

ANNA. Talk.

MATTHEW. Okay.

ANNA. Hang out.

MATTHEW. Cool.

>   *(He walks over to the minibar. Opens it.)*

Drink?

>   *(**ANNA** smiles and rolls her eyes.)*

ANNA. Sure.

>   *(**MATTHEW** tosses her a couple miniatures and she gets some cups. Pours them drinks. Clinks her cup against his.)*

To – whatever this is.

MATTHEW. Yeah.

>   *(Beat.)*

What is this?

ANNA. I don't know. It is what it is.

MATTHEW. You sent me all those e-mails.

ANNA. I was coming to New York and I wanted to see you. So what?

MATTHEW. But it's not like this is the first time you've been here in four years.

ANNA. No.

MATTHEW. So? You never wanted to see me before?

ANNA. It's not that I didn't want to. I just didn't think it would be a good idea.

MATTHEW. Why's it a good idea now?

ANNA. More time has passed. We've moved on. We're not the same people we were before.

MATTHEW. Eh, we are and we aren't.

ANNA. Anyway, it's not like you tried to see me either.

MATTHEW. True. I'm glad I'm seeing you now, though.

ANNA. Me too.

(They drink.)

I like talking to you.

MATTHEW. Me too.

(He smiles.)

ANNA. There's something I wanna ask you, but I don't know if I should.

MATTHEW. Just do it. What could happen?

ANNA. I don't know. I'm scared.

MATTHEW. Well you've got me all the way up here in your hotel room, so if there's something you wanna ask me now would be the time to do it.

(He smiles again, drinks.)

ANNA. Okay.

(Beat.)

Do you see her?

MATTHEW. See who?

ANNA. Emma, Matthew.

(Beat.)

Do you see Emma?

(Energy shift.)

MATTHEW. No. I don't.

ANNA. Do you want to?

MATTHEW. I don't know.

ANNA. Why not?

MATTHEW. I think it would be confusing for her if I were around. I think it would be confusing for Marisol.

ANNA. Marisol said that?

MATTHEW. No, she's never said that. I don't even really talk to her. I don't talk to her, actually.

ANNA. You're allowed to go you know.

MATTHEW. I know.

ANNA. So if you want to, you should.

MATTHEW. Who says I want to?

ANNA. You don't?

MATTHEW. I don't know Anna. I'm not prepared for this conversation.

ANNA. You knew I would ask.

MATTHEW. I honestly had no idea what you were going to say today.

ANNA. Come on.

MATTHEW. Why do you even care anyway?

ANNA. Are you kidding me? Of course I care.

MATTHEW. Okay.

ANNA. I care, Matthew.

MATTHEW. So you care – great, so that's great.

ANNA. Why are you talking to me like this.

MATTHEW. You're the one who made this arrangement, you're the one who left New York, you're the one who got married so quickly and now you seem determined to make sure I know how great your new life is, so yeah, I'm finding your sudden insistence on wanting to know if I have a relationship with her a little bizarre.

ANNA. It's so easy for you to judge right? You think it's so easy. You think I just left and there I am.

MATTHEW. Does he know about her?

ANNA. Don't ask me that.

MATTHEW. Because he doesn't. Because you never told him.

ANNA. Because it doesn't matter, does it?

MATTHEW. Anna.

ANNA. You want me to say horrible things so when I leave you can think horrible things about me.

MATTHEW. No.

ANNA. Yes.

MATTHEW. I'm not the one – /

ANNA. Who what?

MATTHEW. Who didn't want her.

ANNA. We were too young.

MATTHEW. You were out of college. You had a job.

ANNA. I wanted more for her.

MATTHEW. Your parents were younger than we were.

ANNA. And look how that turned out.

MATTHEW. Right. Of course. Typical Anna.

ANNA. I lost her too you know.

MATTHEW. You gave her away.

ANNA. Not because I didn't want her.

MATTHEW. Don't play the grieving one now. You could've had everything – you could've had her, you could've had me – you could've had everything.

ANNA. That isn't true. Stop trying to rewrite it. You were still playing music, you were gone most of the time and you were broke so stop trying to make it seem like you were this thing you are now – you weren't. I was lucky if I saw you once a month.

MATTHEW. But look at what I am now – I could've done it then.

ANNA. Yeah you could've done it and it would've been my fault.

MATTHEW. You rewrite it too.

ANNA. I knew then what I still know now – that it never would've worked. That she would've hated us and we would've hated each other.

MATTHEW. So what are you doing here?

ANNA. I'm at a conference.

MATTHEW. What are you doing here with me? Why did you want to see me so badly?

ANNA. I just did.

MATTHEW. Why?

ANNA. Because I did. Why do I need a reason?

(**MATTHEW** *stares at her.*)

I don't know what to tell you Matthew. I was over it. I really was. I was a different person.

(*Beat.*)

But then recently – I've found myself looking for the two of you in London. Thinking I saw her on the tube. Bringing up conversations about things you like with people who don't even know you. I wasn't lying when I told you I'm happy. But maybe that's not who I am.

(*A knock at the door.*)

Leave it outside, please.

Hungry?

MATTHEW. Are you kidding? No.

ANNA. Me neither. But I think we should try to eat anyway.

MATTHEW. Why?

ANNA. Because if we can't eat...then this all means a lot more than I want it to.

1.4 Later

(**MATTHEW** *and* **ANNA** *hold their stomachs.*)

MATTHEW. Not a good burger.

ANNA. The worst.

MATTHEW. I am in pain.

ANNA. I'm gonna try to go to the bathroom again.

MATTHEW. You might want to light a match first.

ANNA. I can't smell my stomach hurts so bad.

MATTHEW. Just saying.

(**ANNA** *walks to the bathroom and closes the door.*)

(**MATTHEW** *rolls over and sees Anna's purse on the ground. He picks it up, takes out her phone, and looks at it.*)

(**ANNA** *comes out of the bathroom.*)

Better?

ANNA. Kind of.

(**MATTHEW** *holds up the phone.*)

MATTHEW. Who's this?

ANNA. Colin's niece.

MATTHEW. Why do you have her photo as your background?

ANNA. I don't know.

MATTHEW. She's cute.

ANNA. Yeah, we're close.

MATTHEW. Hmm.

ANNA. Scoot over.

(*She lies down next to him.*)

How's your stomach?

MATTHEW. Feels a little better.

(*The phone lights up in his hand. He passes it to* **ANNA.**)

Colin.

(**ANNA** *takes the phone, answers it. Walks toward the bathroom, her back to* **MATTHEW**. *We see her body relax.*)

ANNA. Hello. Hi love. I ate a bad room service burger. No, not food poisoning – just a stomachache. Thanks, I will, thanks. Sorry, I didn't hear it before, it was on silent. It was fine. One good speaker, two kinda meh.

(*She smiles at something he says, an inside joke?*)

Haha, no. She wasn't there. I know! With the sweater and everything.

(*Small beat.*)

Did that meeting go okay? Oh that's great. I knew he'd come around. Okay. Sounds good. I'll call you in the morning. You too. Good night.

(*She hangs up. Walks back over to* **MATTHEW**. *Puts the phone on the nightstand.*)

MATTHEW. Calling to check up on you?

ANNA. To say good night.

MATTHEW. Early for that.

ANNA. Not in London.

MATTHEW. You didn't tell him I was here.

ANNA. He knows we're getting together.

MATTHEW. Does he?

ANNA. Sure.

MATTHEW. If I came to visit you in London would you let me meet him?

ANNA. Why would you want to come visit me in London?

MATTHEW. I'd like to see what your life is like there.

ANNA. I can describe it for you.

MATTHEW. Do it.

ANNA. We live in a nice apartment in Crouch End. I work at the magazine, he's a civil servant. We go to movies and dinners with friends. That's pretty much it.

MATTHEW. When are you going to have kids?

ANNA. We're not.

MATTHEW. Why not?

ANNA. I have a kid.

MATTHEW. Anna –

ANNA. If you have a child and give it away you're not allowed to have another one. It would be wrong.

MATTHEW. Do you really feel that way?

ANNA. Yeah.

MATTHEW. But Anna –

ANNA. What?

MATTHEW. You've always wanted kids.

ANNA. I know.

MATTHEW. You love kids.

ANNA. I know.

MATTHEW. And you're not going to have any?

ANNA. I have one.

MATTHEW. She doesn't count.

ANNA. How can you say she doesn't count, of course she counts.

MATTHEW. You know what I mean. She doesn't know who you are.

ANNA. Let's say one day she finds out – she doesn't look like Marisol and she doesn't look like Ted and she's curious. She wants to know why her parents are so much older than everyone else's. Or maybe she finds some letter or document, or maybe she gets sick and they need something from me. But somehow she finds out. And she finds me.

If I have other kids, if I have kids I kept and didn't keep her – no, no I wouldn't do that to her.

MATTHEW. But Anna –

ANNA. Don't think I haven't thought about this.

MATTHEW. So what if you hadn't had her?

ANNA. What about it?

MATTHEW. You would've had other kids then.

ANNA. Probably.

MATTHEW. I don't understand that.

ANNA. Not having her was never an option.

MATTHEW. The Catholic Atheist strikes again.

ANNA. Agnostic.

MATTHEW. Semantics. Does Colin want kids?

ANNA. Yes.

MATTHEW. How do you handle that?

ANNA. He wants me more.

MATTHEW. You weren't this confident when we were together.

(**ANNA** *gives a little laugh.*)

What?

ANNA. Oh honey, how could anyone be confident with you?

1.5 Later

(**ANNA** *and* **MATTHEW** *sit on the floor, drinking and laughing; empty miniatures are all around them.*)

MATTHEW. And then you said to him, I will not leave I paid you for a drink and I want you to give me that drink – and he looked at you like you were crazy like who the hell does this petite little girl think she is?

ANNA. I doubt that bartender would've used the word petite.

MATTHEW. Why?

ANNA. He would have said skinny. He would have said skinny little girl.

MATTHEW. I guess it's what he would have *thought* anyway because he didn't say shit.

ANNA. Nope – just gave me my drink.

MATTHEW. You were lucky you didn't get punched.

ANNA. Please, no one was going to punch me.

MATTHEW. We were in a dive in Memphis.

ANNA. You were so surprised when I showed up there.

MATTHEW. Yeah because I didn't want you to come.

ANNA. And Gigi was there.

MATTHEW. Can we not?

ANNA. Slut.

MATTHEW. Don't talk about her like that.

ANNA. I forgot that she was there. I forgot she saw that whole thing – somehow it doesn't seem as funny now.

MATTHEW. Can you just stop, we were having a nice time.

ANNA. We were, weren't we?

MATTHEW. Yeah.

ANNA. Those tours were fun.

MATTHEW. No they weren't. They were awful.

ANNA. I know they were awful but weren't they also kind of fun?

MATTHEW. I guess, if you just flew in and flew out for a couple of days, like you did, then they were. But being in the van with the guys all the time – it was hard not to kill yourself.

ANNA. Don't you miss it?

MATTHEW. Not really.

ANNA. You really like gardening?

MATTHEW. Back then I had no resume and a band that was just successful enough for me to pretend it was a career.

ANNA. It was a career.

MATTHEW. How long can that last though?

ANNA. You'll never know – you cut it short.

MATTHEW. Anna, come on.

ANNA. It just makes me sad I guess.

MATTHEW. Fucking typical.

ANNA. Excuse me?

MATTHEW. We break up because you can't handle the band life – now I have a regular life – like Colin – and you think it's sad.

ANNA. Is that a joke? You think the reason we broke up was because I couldn't handle you being in a band?

MATTHEW. That's not what I said.

ANNA. We broke up because Tommy died and you basically left me alone and stopped talking to me.

MATTHEW. That was a complicated time. You know that. I was fucked up.

ANNA. I know. I'm not blaming you. I just don't think it's fair to say that we broke up because you were in a band. You were in a band the whole time we were together.

MATTHEW. It's also not fair for you to hold me to this standard of who you expect me to be for the rest of my life.

ANNA. I'm not doing that.

MATTHEW. And while we're on the subject don't forget that you didn't even tell me you were pregnant until almost the end.

ANNA. Because you were gone that whole time.

MATTHEW. And you didn't want to have a kid with a guy in a band.

ANNA. And I didn't want to have a kid with someone who was so far removed from me emotionally that I could barely have a conversation with you.

MATTHEW. You made up your mind about what you wanted to do and told me after. I never had a choice.

ANNA. You made your choice when you checked out of our relationship.

MATTHEW. You're talking about the month my best friend died. You're not talking about a normal time in our lives.

ANNA. He was my friend too. I was in that car too. That's something we should have been able to get through together. But if going away was more important or what you needed, I wasn't going to use being pregnant to make you stay.

MATTHEW. Well, maybe you should've.

ANNA. That's unfair and you know it. You didn't want to stay. You didn't want me to make you stay. You would've hated me if I did that. I would've hated me if I did that. You wanted to leave. You needed to be playing music – it saved you.

MATTHEW. Don't say that. That's trite. That's gross.

ANNA. No. Fuck you, that's what happened and now after all of that, after what all of us went through and you're not even playing? You're a fucking gardener. Are you kidding me? That sucks, Matthew. And yeah, it makes me really fucking sad.

MATTHEW. Well I guess you're entitled to your opinion.

ANNA. Fine, you know what, never mind. Be a gardener. I don't care. What does your life have to do with me anymore, anyway?

MATTHEW. Fuck you for saying that.

ANNA. I mean it. You're right. We broke up because I was never going to be happy with you. We were never going to work. Even when we were together and things were good I came in second to Tommy. I always knew that. I flew in and out but Tommy had you all the time. And now that he's gone and you've quit you want to pretend like it wasn't that important.

Get over yourself, Matthew, you're not happy being a gardener. Fuck playing? Fuck music? Yeah right. That's who you were.

MATTHEW. Yeah, well I was you / too.

ANNA. But giving it up and then blaming me – when I'm gone, when I've been gone – when I'm married –

MATTHEW. I love that you can always fall on that, put that guard up – how could I be hurt or hurt someone when I'm *married* –

ANNA. I don't do that.

MATTHEW. How could anything that happened to us have affected me when I was able to *marry* so quickly –

ANNA. Stop it.

MATTHEW. Want to know what everyone thinks of your marriage?

ANNA. Don't

MATTHEW. They think it's a joke. They think you lost your fucking mind. They think you still love me – that you'll always love me and that Colin is a wet blanket.

ANNA. They. They is you.

MATTHEW. They is you, Anna. Tell me you love Colin the way that you loved me –

ANNA. I don't have to prove anything to you.

MATTHEW. Just say it.

ANNA. I'm happy.

MATTHEW. Happy is not what I'm asking you. It's not the same thing.

ANNA. You're right – it's better.

MATTHEW. How can you live with yourself?

ANNA. How can you? Tell me you love gardening.

MATTHEW. I never claimed to. I didn't marry it.

ANNA. Very mature.

MATTHEW. What do you think about before you go to sleep? Do you think about me and you?

ANNA. Sometimes.

MATTHEW. I do, every night.

ANNA. That is not true.

MATTHEW. How do you know?

ANNA. It might be true in this moment but it's not really true. Nothing you said was backed up. You loved me the most one day and Gigi the most the next and probably a slew of other girls I never even knew about. You don't see past the first grabbable emotion.

MATTHEW. I know what I feel.

ANNA. Yeah and that's all.

MATTHEW. What do you want from me?

ANNA. I don't want anything from you. I made that very clear when I left and yes – *married* someone else.

MATTHEW. Here we go again.

ANNA. The truth is in actions not feelings.

MATTHEW. Do you have that embroidered on a pillow?

ANNA. Fuck you.

> (**MATTHEW** *kisses her and she kisses him back; they go to the bed.*)

1.6 Later

(It's just after.)

*(**ANNA** looks over at **MATTHEW**.)*

ANNA. You have Gigi's name tattooed on your back?

MATTHEW. Yeah.

ANNA. When did you get that?

MATTHEW. I don't know. A while ago.

ANNA. Do you still see her?

MATTHEW. Yeah.

ANNA. Typical.

MATTHEW. What's typical?

ANNA. That she of all people has staying power.

MATTHEW. Don't dismiss her, I'm sick of you dismissing her.

ANNA. How nice to be able to defend the woman you cheated on me with.

MATTHEW. Yeah and I also cheated on her with you so what's the fucking difference?

ANNA. Um – excuse me, when did you cheat on her with me?

MATTHEW. Oh about five minutes ago.

ANNA. You're still together?

MATTHEW. Yup.

ANNA. And you just now thought to tell me this?

MATTHEW. Didn't come up before.

ANNA. Jesus fucking Christ.

(She quickly puts her clothes on.)

MATTHEW. So now you're Mother Teresa?

ANNA. You are a filthy disgusting asshole pig.

MATTHEW. How am I any worse than you? If anything I'm better. You're married.

ANNA. Gigi? You and Gigi? I'm fucking speechless.

MATTHEW. Come on – you knew there was someone.

ANNA. Sure – some gardening floozy, some intern, anyone. Gigi?!

(She puts her head in her hands.)

MATTHEW. Stop it. Stop this shit, I'm not going through this same shit with you – again.

ANNA. You really know how to hurt me.

MATTHEW. Gigi thought you were brilliant and you shit all over her – I'm not apologizing to you.

ANNA. Gigi was trying to fuck my boyfriend so I wasn't really interested in her compliments.

MATTHEW. You humiliated her every chance you got.

ANNA. She was an idiot.

MATTHEW. She was shy.

ANNA. She's probably still an idiot.

MATTHEW. And you're still a stuck-up bitch.

ANNA. That's great, insult me to avoid talking about her.

MATTHEW. I'm not avoiding talking about her.

ANNA. Fine – do you love her?

MATTHEW. Yes.

ANNA. It's that easy to admit, huh?

MATTHEW. Why shouldn't it be?

ANNA. I can't believe you.

MATTHEW. Just because you refuse to say it.

ANNA. I do not.

MATTHEW. Colin – you refuse to say it about Colin.

ANNA. He's my husband of course I love him.

MATTHEW. He's not your husband.

ANNA. What are you talking about?

MATTHEW. I'm your husband. I always have been. I know it and you do too. I always was and I always will be. He's just – legally bound to you.

ANNA. And you're just nothing to me.

MATTHEW. Not true, not true.

ANNA. This was a mistake.

MATTHEW. This was your idea.

ANNA. I know, but it was a mistake.

MATTHEW. I'm glad you suggested it.

ANNA. Why?

MATTHEW. Because I need to talk to you about something.

ANNA. About what?

MATTHEW. I think you should have a baby with Colin.

ANNA. What?

MATTHEW. I think it would be good for you.

ANNA. I'm not going to do that.

MATTHEW. You always wanted to be a mother.

ANNA. I am a mother.

MATTHEW. I want you to go home and I want you to think about what I said. I'm looking out for you now. You're not going to be happy writing articles about makeup forever.

ANNA. I don't write the articles.

MATTHEW. Whatever it is you do.

ANNA. You think you know what's best for me and you're not even interested in who I am.

MATTHEW. What you do isn't who you are.

ANNA. No, especially not in your case.

MATTHEW. I don't know why you can't seem to understand this – I like what I do now. I'm good at it. I need what it affords me.

ANNA. Ha. What exactly does it *afford* you?

MATTHEW. Money – stability. I'm making plans, Anna.

ANNA. What plans could you possibly be making? Please don't tell me that you're thinking of marrying Gigi.

MATTHEW. No.

ANNA. Thank god.

MATTHEW. But we are living together.

ANNA. Well, that doesn't mean anything to me.

MATTHEW. I didn't think it would.

ANNA. You're incapable of ever really committing to anything.

MATTHEW. That's not what I said.

ANNA. And I would hardly consider moving in with Gigi to be news.

MATTHEW. We've been living together for years.

ANNA. Could've told me in a postcard.

MATTHEW. You're missing the point.

ANNA. Sorry, what was the point?

MATTHEW. We're going to get her.

ANNA. What?

MATTHEW. I'm going to get her.

ANNA. Who?

MATTHEW. You know who. I'm taking her with me.

ANNA. Taking her where?

MATTHEW. Here. For good. She's coming to live with me here. I'm going to tell her.

ANNA. Tell her what –

MATTHEW. Everything – She's going to know who I am.

ANNA. You can't do that!

MATTHEW. I can, Anna.

ANNA. No you can't. There are papers.

MATTHEW. Papers you signed. I never did.

ANNA. But –

MATTHEW. You never listed me as her father. I never signed anything.

ANNA. She's too young.

MATTHEW. She'll be okay.

ANNA. She's too young to be able to handle this.

MATTHEW. She'll be fine.

ANNA. What about Marisol? She'll fight you.

MATTHEW. Marisol can stay in her life.

ANNA. You're just trying to hurt me. This is all just to hurt me, isn't it?

MATTHEW. This is to have a life with my daughter. The daughter you didn't want.

ANNA. You didn't want her either.

MATTHEW. I couldn't handle her then – now I can.

ANNA. I'll fight you.

MATTHEW. You have no rights. Your husband doesn't know she exists. Are you going to ruin your perfect life over this?

ANNA. I don't want you to do this. I don't want it. Please I don't want her life to be like this –

MATTHEW. Like what?

ANNA. I want her to live in Princeton with Marisol and Ted. I want her to go to ballet class and eat carrot sticks after school.

MATTHEW. You think I don't know how to cut up a carrot?

ANNA. I think you won't.

MATTHEW. You can't control her life.

ANNA. I don't want her raised by Gigi. I want her to be smart.

MATTHEW. There you go again.

ANNA. I don't care who you fuck but I don't want my daughter's mother to be a woman who doesn't read.

MATTHEW. She reads.

ANNA. I'm not talking about magazines.

MATTHEW. Funny, coming from you.

ANNA. What can I do to talk you out of this?

MATTHEW. There's nothing you can do. I'm at a point in my life where I want a family. And I'm not willing to pretend I don't already have one.

ANNA. You don't have one. That family doesn't exist.

MATTHEW. Just because you want to pretend it didn't happen.

ANNA. I cannot believe you would do that to her.

MATTHEW. What? Love her.

ANNA. Ruin her.

MATTHEW. This conversation is over.

(He walks to the door.)

ANNA. You can't leave now.

MATTHEW. Why not?

ANNA. You can't drop this on me and then leave.

MATTHEW. Sure I can, I can do anything I want.

ANNA. You're only thinking about yourself.

MATTHEW. Well I'm sure as hell not thinking about you.

ANNA. You're not thinking of her. She's happy. She's adjusted.

MATTHEW. How would you know? You don't see her, you don't know how she is –

ANNA. I know how children are and I know that a four-year-old is not going to like being taken from her mom and her life and her nice suburban home and being dropped in a shitty apartment in the city with a new father and some woman.

MATTHEW. I would've killed to know who my birth parents were, I would've done anything.

ANNA. Not when you were four –

MATTHEW. If I'd known when I was four –

ANNA. You love your parents.

MATTHEW. If they'd told me when I was four.

ANNA. Who would tell a four-year-old that?! Only an imbecile – you will mess her up forever.

MATTHEW. So they told me when I was eighteen and you think I'm not messed up because of that?

ANNA. It would've been different.

MATTHEW. Yeah – maybe I could've been happy.

ANNA. It would have been a different kind of void, a harder one to fill –

MATTHEW. Like you know anything about it.

ANNA. I do know something about it.

MATTHEW. How could you?

ANNA. I dropped her off to Marisol didn't I? I was with you when you tried to find your birth parents.

MATTHEW. And that makes you an expert.

ANNA. I'm not telling you not to do it – clearly that's not going to work. I'm just telling you to wait – just four more years at eight she'll be better able / to –

MATTHEW. Better able to hate me right? That's what you're hoping? That she'll want to stay with Marisol and have a voice to express it?

ANNA. If you take a four-year-old away from her home –

MATTHEW. She gets over it.

> (ANNA *goes into the bathroom and shuts the door. She stays in there for a while.* MATTHEW *sits on the bed. He picks up Anna's phone again.*)
>
> (*He looks to the bathroom door.*)

How long you gonna stay in there?

> (*No response.*)

This girl's pretty cute. Your niece.

> (ANNA *comes out of the bathroom.*)

ANNA. Put it back, okay?

MATTHEW. I'm just saying – she's cute.

> (*Beat.*)

ANNA. I wish you wouldn't. That's all I can say I guess.

> (MATTHEW *softens. He tries to take her hand.*)

Don't touch me.

MATTHEW. Anna... I didn't come here to hurt you.

ANNA. I have a question.

MATTHEW. Okay.

ANNA. I asked you here.

MATTHEW. Uh-huh.

ANNA. So.

MATTHEW. I don't know what the question is.

ANNA. I'm the one who wanted to see you.

MATTHEW. I know.

ANNA. So when were you planning on telling me all of this?

MATTHEW. I was going to.

ANNA. When?

MATTHEW. When – I had it more figured out.

ANNA. What does that mean?

MATTHEW. I mean, I've thought about it before and then when you wanted to meet me I thought when am I going to have a chance to see her in person again and then it all just kind of came out.

(**ANNA** *laughs, a relieved laugh.*)

What are you doing?

ANNA. Oh my god. I thought you were serious.

MATTHEW. I am serious.

(**ANNA** *laughs.*)

ANNA. And I believed you, my god.

MATTHEW. Stop it.

(**ANNA** *looks at him.*)

ANNA. You're not going to do anything, Matthew.

MATTHEW. I am not joking about this.

ANNA. Oh I know you're not joking, but that anything will actually come of this – except maybe an awkward conversation with Marisol – No, no – this too shall pass. I bet you don't even have a lawyer.

MATTHEW. Not yet.

ANNA. Oh honey – you thought this was going to be so easy. I feel almost bad for you.

(*Beat.*)

Do you want me to tell you what's going to happen when you leave here?

MATTHEW. ...

ANNA. You are going to go home and get in bed with Gigi. She'll know you've been with another woman – but won't know it's me so she won't say anything. Tomorrow you'll think long and hard about tonight and you'll still be set on going through with it. You'll tell Gigi you have news. She'll cry and break something because the last thing she wants in her apartment, is a living reminder

of me. Still sure of your decision you'll call Marisol –
say you've had an epiphany – that you've come to a
certain point in your life. She'll be polite but have no
idea what you're talking about. And then, while you're
talking you'll hear her in the background – maybe
she'll be eating her dinner and complaining about the
vegetables, maybe its a kids' show she's watching or
maybe you hear her giggling in the bathtub but you
will hear something and in that moment you'll realize
you can't do it – that you were never going to be able to
do it and that's why we made this decision in the first
place.

> (**MATTHEW** *is silent.*)

MATTHEW. I was wrong about something too.

ANNA. What was that?

MATTHEW. I always thought you'd be such a good mother.

> (*He puts his coat on and walks to the door.
> He exits.*)

> (**ANNA** *sits.*)

> (*After a moment, she picks up the phone and
> dials.*)

ANNA. Hi. It's Anna. I'm in town.

ACT II

2.1 Princeton

*(**ANNA** sits in Marisol's living room. There is nothing out of place except for a pink toy on the floor. **ANNA** sits in a chair, transfixed by the toy – she stares at it.)*

*(**MARISOL** enters with a cup of tea; she hands it to **ANNA**.)*

MARISOL. I didn't know if you took milk.

ANNA. No, thank you.

MARISOL. We do have some, if you'd like it.

ANNA. This will be fine.

*(**MARISOL** sits.)*

MARISOL. It's nice to see you.

ANNA. You too.

MARISOL. We like your letters.

ANNA. Oh.

MARISOL. I read them to her.

ANNA. You do.

MARISOL. Yes.

ANNA. And who do you tell her they're from?

MARISOL. We say they are from her pen pal.

ANNA. Ah.

MARISOL. She looks forward to them.

ANNA. I like writing them.

*(She looks back at the toy. **MARISOL** puts it away.)*

MARISOL. You try to keep the house, you know. Things get messy.

ANNA. It looks wonderful.

MARISOL. Thank you.

ANNA. I've always loved this house.

MARISOL. I hope you're not disappointed?

ANNA. Disappointed?

MARISOL. That she's not here.

ANNA. No, no. I wasn't expecting.

MARISOL. There's a pool nearby. Our neighbors have a little girl too so they took them both.

ANNA. She swims?

MARISOL. She loves it. They have these classes at the pool. Little fishes it's called. When you move up, you get to be a shark.

ANNA. Oh.

MARISOL. I just thought it might be better – less confusing for her, to be out.

ANNA. I agree.

(*Beat.*)

ANNA.	**MARISOL**.
I wanted to say –	Are you sure you are okay with just that tea? We have cookies.

ANNA. Just tea. Marisol, I just wanted to say how grateful – /

MARISOL. No, no. Anna please don't.

ANNA. I want to.

MARISOL. It's unnecessary. I've always told you that.

ANNA. But I just wanted to.

MARISOL. I am more than happy to – she's a blessing.

ANNA. At your age to take on – /

MARISOL. She makes me feel young.

ANNA. That's just, I'm just so happy she's here with you and Ted. Where is Ted, by the way?

MARISOL. Traveling. You know how much he works.

ANNA. Yes.

(**MARISOL** *squeezes* **ANNA***'s hand.*)

MARISOL. I want to talk about you.

ANNA. I'm not much to talk about.

MARISOL. Nonsense. Your fancy career. Your beautiful husband.

ANNA. Yeah, he's attractive.

MARISOL. How are things across the pond?

ANNA. They're good.

MARISOL. How's the magazine?

ANNA. Good.

MARISOL. And life, other than work?

ANNA. It's all good. Steady and you know, good.

MARISOL. I pray for you.

ANNA. Thank you.

MARISOL. I hope you can feel it, from all the way over here.

ANNA. I think I do.

MARISOL. It's been a long time since I've seen you. You are just as beautiful as ever.

(**ANNA** *puts her cup down.*)

ANNA. Marisol.

MARISOL. Yes?

ANNA. What do you...

MARISOL. Yes?

ANNA. What do you think of me?

MARISOL. I don't understand.

ANNA. How after all this, do you still see me as... After what I've done?

MARISOL. I thought there might be some of this when you called.

(**ANNA** *looks around.*)

ANNA. This is the kind of house I wish I grew up in. It makes me sad sitting here.

MARISOL. Anna...

ANNA. Does she hate me? If she knew me, would she hate me?

MARISOL. No one blames you, Anna. I certainly don't blame you. And Emma – Emma is just fine.

ANNA. Will you tell me about her? Will you tell me what she likes?

MARISOL. Are you sure you're up for this?

ANNA. I just want to know who she is.

MARISOL. I can show you things, if you think that would be okay. I have some artwork – some things she's made at school.

ANNA. I'd like that.

MARISOL. Okay. I'll be right back.

> (*She exits. After a few beats she comes back with an album.*)

ANNA. You made an album of it?

MARISOL. Just so it doesn't get lost.

ANNA. These are...

MARISOL. Well you know, it's kid stuff. But I like them.

ANNA. They're beautiful.

MARISOL. See this one? It's a person. You can see the head and the arms, legs. It seems silly to say, but for a four-year-old, it's quite good.

ANNA. Is that you?

MARISOL. Oh who knows, it's just a figure. A blob.

ANNA. I like these.

MARISOL. Yes, she really likes to draw trains. She's a bit of a tomboy that way.

ANNA. Only that way though, as far as I can see.

MARISOL. You mean the pink? Yeah, pink is her thing.

ANNA. She seems like a very happy little girl.

MARISOL. She's sweet. My sweet girl.

ANNA. Yes.

MARISOL. Oh, I didn't –

ANNA. No, that's what I wanted to hear. *Your sweet girl.*

MARISOL. I'm sorry, Anna. If this is too difficult.

ANNA. No, no. This is *exactly* why I wanted to come.

(She smiles at **MARISOL.***)*

What time did you say she was getting back?

MARISOL. Well I just have to call the neighbor...he said she could have supper with them.

ANNA. I want you to promise me that you're not going to let anything happen to her.

MARISOL. If you're worried about our neighbor we've known him forever.

ANNA. I don't mean that. You know I trust you. I mean... I mean...

MARISOL. Yes?

ANNA. I mean if Matthew were to get in touch with you? If he were to try something *disruptive...*

MARISOL. Has something happened?

ANNA. What if Matthew wanted her back?

(Beat.)

I saw him and he said something. I don't even know if he would. But if he did. We need to have a plan. Legally I don't think he can. Well, I don't really know actually and that's what scares me. But I want you to be on guard. Have your lawyer ready.

MARISOL. Anna. Didn't you know this day was coming?

ANNA. What?

MARISOL. I love that little girl. I love her with my whole heart.

ANNA. I know.

MARISOL. But I knew when you came here with her in your arms and that look on your face –

ANNA. You knew that she was yours now. Your sweet girl.

MARISOL. I knew that this wouldn't be forever.

ANNA. No. Marisol. This is not what I came to talk about.

MARISOL. You were so rash. When you were pregnant – and you wouldn't even tell your family.

ANNA. You are my family.

MARISOL. Your real family, Anna.

ANNA. Who are you if not my family?

MARISOL. You know we've always loved you. But that doesn't make us your history, honey.

ANNA. Who cares about history. It's the future that's important.

MARISOL. History's all I've got.

ANNA. You mean Tommy?

MARISOL. I wish people would let me talk about him. Everyone wants me to push it under the rug. It upsets them, you know? Even Ted. He doesn't want to talk about it. Even you –

ANNA. What can I say?

MARISOL. It couldn't have been easy on him. Always being the third wheel like that with you and Matthew. No wonder he drank.

ANNA. He did a little more than drink.

MARISOL. And you were flawless?

ANNA. We all made mistakes back then. But can we talk about Emma?

MARISOL. It's always about Emma. It's never about Tommy.

ANNA. Emma is a child. And Tommy was – he was an adult.

MARISOL. Tommy was my child. And I get tired, Anna. I get tired of you pretending like this whole thing has nothing to do with him.

(*Beat.*)

We should consider what Matthew is proposing.

ANNA. I can't.

MARISOL. Ted's sick.

ANNA. What?

MARISOL. He has colon cancer.

ANNA. Oh my god.

MARISOL. So soon – I'm going to need to start taking care of him. I'm not saying she can't stay. Of course I'm not. But – how it's been. How we've all been. That's not going to stay the same. Do you understand? I'm going to need help.

ANNA. I can help.

MARISOL. You can't. Not from over there.

ANNA. I'm sorry about Ted.

MARISOL. I think, I hate to say it, he's almost relieved. He knows he's going to get me back now.

ANNA. What do you mean?

MARISOL. I've been distracted. Emma takes up most of my time and I haven't been a very good wife. He's been traveling more than ever – even after the diagnosis...

ANNA. He's a hard worker.

MARISOL. He never thought it was a good idea, you know. He loves her, sure, the way you love a pet I think. But he never wanted us to take her in. He said we were too old. That she wouldn't replace Tommy and it was stupid of me to think that. But I never thought that – I just wanted to help.

ANNA. I wasn't trying to replace him.

MARISOL. Oh, of course you were. It was a consolation prize. Your baby for mine.

ANNA. That's twisted, Marisol. That's sick. You must think I'm really sick.

MARISOL. It's always about you and what people think of you. You know Ted never liked Tommy running around with all of you. That's not how you handle a problem like Tommy he said, you don't stick him with a bunch of other Tommys.

ANNA. What do you want me to say? That I'm sorry? Of course I am. I'm sorry for all of it. I'm sorry Tommy died and I'm sorry the circumstances of Emma's birth were the way they were but I'm not a selfish person. I just wanted what was best for her.

MARISOL. Everyone is selfish, Anna. There's no reason denying it. When Tommy died you probably thought, "Thank god it wasn't Matthew."

ANNA. Maybe it should have been me. Then you wouldn't have to worry about me – or Emma.

MARISOL. Let's not talk about it anymore. It's just upsetting both of us.

ANNA. Don't you love her, Marisol?

MARISOL. Of course I do.

ANNA. So fight for her. She needs you.

(**MARISOL** *looks at the clock.*)

MARISOL. You should go. She's going to be home soon.

ANNA. Please don't make me beg.

(*She starts to tremble.*)

I don't know how I'm going to do this.

MARISOL. Oh hell, wait here.

(*She exits.* **ANNA** *tries to calm herself down.*)

(*After a minute or so,* **MARISOL** *enters and hands* **ANNA** *a fancy pillbox.*)

Cut these in half, quarters even. And don't drink when you're on them. These are not for daily use, do you understand?

ANNA. What are these?

MARISOL. You're not the only one, Anna, who's been dealing with a lot.

2.2 New York

(**ANNA** *and* **GIGI** *sit in a café.*)

ANNA. Thanks for meeting with me.

GIGI. Uh-huh.

ANNA. I'm sure you were surprised when I called.

GIGI. Yeah.

ANNA. We've never exactly been friends.

GIGI. No.

ANNA. So, thanks.

GIGI. I was curious.

ANNA. Right. Why would I be calling you?

GIGI. Yeah.

ANNA. After all this time...

GIGI. Yes.

(*Pause.*)

So?

ANNA. So.

GIGI. Why are you?

ANNA. I just wanted you to know that you have my blessing.

GIGI. I don't need your blessing.

ANNA. Oh god. You don't think I'm talking about Matthew? Of course you don't need my blessing. I would never... how rude you must think I am. Gigi.

I was talking about Emma.

GIGI. Sorry?

ANNA. Matthew told me about your plans...to go get her. And I want you to know, you have my blessing.

GIGI. You saw Matthew?

ANNA. He didn't tell you?

GIGI. No, he must've.

ANNA. Don't worry it was nothing.

GIGI. Nothing?

ANNA. Nothing happened I mean. We mostly just talked about Emma.

GIGI. Emma?

ANNA. Our daughter.

GIGI. Daughter?

ANNA. Mine and Matthew's.

GIGI. You have a – /

ANNA. Please tell me you knew about Emma.

GIGI. I – /

ANNA. I would hate to think Matthew's been keeping her a secret. Especially since he's planning to have her come live with you.

GIGI. Where is she?

ANNA. She's with Tommy's mother.

GIGI. Marisol?

ANNA. You know Marisol?

>   (**GIGI** gives **ANNA** a look.)

Sorry. I guess I forget how much you were around in those days. Emma lives with Marisol.

GIGI. When?

ANNA. When did I have her?

>   (**GIGI** nods.)

Just before I moved to London. And just before, I suppose, you and Matthew got together. Does that timing sound right to you? Four, five years?

>   (**GIGI** picks up her pack of cigarettes with
>   shaky hands, takes one out and tries to light
>   it.)

Gigi. You can't smoke in here.

>   (**GIGI** puts down the cigarette and picks up a
>   glass of water. She spills a little.)

>   (**ANNA** mops it up.)

Gigi. Look at me. I never would have come here if I thought you didn't already know. I only asked you to meet me here because I thought I was doing the right thing.

GIGI. I have to go.

(She tries to get up from the table, but her bag is caught on the chair.)

ANNA. Are you okay?

(She tries to help untangle the bag. GIGI does it herself and moves away from ANNA.)

GIGI. I don't need your help.

(She exits.)

(ANNA sits at the table, staring.)

2.3 London

*(**MATTHEW** is in Anna and Colin's flat. He looks at their pictures. **COLIN** enters and hands **MATTHEW** a drink.)*

COLIN. So here you are.

MATTHEW. Here I am.

COLIN. Thought you'd turn up sooner or later.

MATTHEW. You did?

COLIN. Course. All that nonsense between you and Anna. You were bound to.

MATTHEW. So you know about me and Anna then?

COLIN. Which part? The little fling in New York?

MATTHEW. She told you about that?

COLIN. Surprised?

MATTHEW. Kind of.

COLIN. I'm not intimidated by you or your history with my wife so let's get that out of the way right from the start.

MATTHEW. Good.

COLIN. Is it?

MATTHEW. Yes.

COLIN. And here I thought you'd come to compare cocks.

MATTHEW. No.

COLIN. What then?

MATTHEW. I've had some free time recently since my girlfriend's left me –

COLIN. Sorry to hear that.

MATTHEW. Yeah well, them's the breaks. Anyway I thought, you know I've never been to London.

COLIN. Not even in your glory days?

MATTHEW. You never really see a city when you're touring.

COLIN. You want to go to Big Ben? Is that it? London Tower.

MATTHEW. Exactly.

COLIN. Anna's not here.

MATTHEW. No?

COLIN. Paris. Fashion Week.

MATTHEW. You didn't want to tag alone? Hang out with the models.

COLIN. Not my speed, that. Need a refill?

MATTHEW. Thanks.

(**COLIN** *refills* **MATTHEW**'s *glass.*)

COLIN. Where are you staying?

MATTHEW. Not sure.

COLIN. Surely you've booked a room.

MATTHEW. Actually I just went to the airport and got on a plane.

COLIN. Expensive, that route.

MATTHEW. My business is doing well.

COLIN. Yes, yes the rockin' gardener.

MATTHEW. People will pay a lot for a fantasy.

COLIN. You consider yourself a fantasy then?

MATTHEW. To some people, but not to Anna.

COLIN. I'd say, precisely to Anna.

MATTHEW. How'd you get her to tell you about us? About our –

COLIN. Transgression.

MATTHEW. If that's what you want to call it.

You push her?

COLIN. No, mate. I don't believe in pushing a woman around. She told me because we have a mutual respect for one another.

MATTHEW. She's got a funny way of showing it.

COLIN. Right so was there anything else then? Or did you just come here to drink my liquor and insult my wife?

MATTHEW. You two don't seem to have any secrets.

COLIN. No big ones.

MATTHEW. That's admirable.

COLIN. We think so.

(He takes **MATTHEW***'s glass.)*

COLIN. Thank you so much for stopping by.

MATTHEW. You'll tell Anna I was here?

COLIN. Listen, Matthew. I'm not going to pretend you and Anna didn't have something. You did. But that's over now. It's time to move on.

MATTHEW. If you say so.

COLIN. I'll tell her you came by.

MATTHEW. Thanks.

COLIN. I'm sorry about your girlfriend.

MATTHEW. Yeah, you know. Shit happens.

COLIN. Eloquently put.

MATTHEW. There is one more thing if you don't mind.

(He takes a large envelope out of his jacket.)

Can you give this to her?

COLIN. Course.

MATTHEW. And because of that mutual respect you mentioned I can assume you won't look at it before you do.

COLIN. Right.

(He walks **MATTHEW** *to the door.)*

MATTHEW. Oh. And will you tell Anna that she can stop laughing now, because I'm fucking serious.

(He exits.)

2.4 Later

(**ANNA** and **COLIN** are in their living room, talking.)

COLIN. A child. You have a child. And you were never going to tell me?

ANNA. I didn't want you to think...

COLIN. You only had her six months before we met. And you're walking around London like it's nothing – just another happy-go-lucky American abroad.

ANNA. I was trying to move on. I didn't want to think about it. I didn't want to hurt you –

COLIN. You didn't want to hurt me? Or maybe, you didn't want me to hurt you. Because I don't think I would have been so kind to a woman who'd just abandoned her daughter.

(**ANNA** hardens.)

ANNA. Yeah, you're right. You probably wouldn't have.

(Beat.)

But you were very nice to a woman who was in love with someone else.

COLIN. Ah. Is that what we're back to?

ANNA. No. I'm sorry. I shouldn't have said that. Colin, he doesn't mean anything to me now, you know that.

COLIN. What about her though? What about the daughter you had with him? How can I dismiss him like he's nothing when he's the father of your child?

ANNA. You can because –

(She's never said this out loud before.)

Because he's not the father.

COLIN. What?

ANNA. He thinks he is, but he's not.

COLIN. Jesus. How many boulders are going to fall on my head today? Who is he?

ANNA. Who?

COLIN. Him, Anna! Jesus. What is the matter with you? The father.

ANNA. Oh, he was my friend. Our friend.

COLIN. Your friend, right. And I thought Matthew was the only man from your past I had to worry about.

ANNA. Well, you don't have to worry about Tommy because he's dead.

COLIN. Tommy. Of course, my wife the groupie.

ANNA. I wasn't a groupie. It wasn't like that. I wasn't some hanger-on. They were my family. And I was never in love with him. So you don't have to get possessive with me. I just messed up once. Tommy was sick. He was a very sick boy.

COLIN. What does that mean?

ANNA. He was anxious and worked up and he was my friend so I was trying to calm him down and something happened that should never have happened.

COLIN. Hell of a fucking nurse you were.

ANNA. He wasn't well, Colin. He would have hurt himself and I needed him to slow down – /

COLIN. Slow down and what? Fuck you?

ANNA. It was only one time.

COLIN. When you were with Matthew? The love of your life. The man I've had to compare myself to all these years. And you couldn't even be faithful to *him*.

ANNA. Colin. It so wasn't like that.

COLIN. What happened?

ANNA. I told you he died. A car accident. You know that already. Except. Matthew and I were in the car too.

(*She pulls back her hair and points to a small scar.*)

I didn't fall out of a tree when I was six. That was a lie.

COLIN. What else? What else have you been lying about?

ANNA. It doesn't matter.

COLIN. It does. I want to know everything you've been hiding from me.

ANNA. I don't want to talk about it.

COLIN. Too bad. You're going to talk about it!

(He stops, he doesn't like himself like this.)

Sorry.

(He takes a breath. Tries again.)

Darling. I thought we were going to know each other completely.

ANNA. You can't know anyone completely. That should be obvious to us by now. I don't want to pretend anymore.

COLIN. Come on, darling. This will help. The talking cure. I won't be mad, I promise. I'm sorry I yelled. Just start the story from the beginning. Tell me what happened.

2.5 Princeton

(**GIGI** *waits with* **MARISOL** *at her house.*)

MARISOL. You don't talk much do you?

GIGI. Not really.

MARISOL. That's okay.

GIGI. I'm not dumb.

MARISOL. Of course you're not.

GIGI. I know people think that. I'm not. I have lots of thoughts. Good ones.

MARISOL. I don't think you're dumb.

GIGI. And I care about stuff.

(**MARISOL** *is quiet.*)

Did you know Matthew when he was a kid?

MARISOL. No, he went to college with my son.

GIGI. Oh.

MARISOL. I knew Anna.

GIGI. Oh.

MARISOL. Her family lived close by, but then they moved to Seattle when she was a teenager.

GIGI. Were she and Tommy friends?

MARISOL. Yes, but they were young.

GIGI. So you love Anna.

MARISOL. Why do you say that?

GIGI. You've known her such a long time. You must love her, right?

MARISOL. I would do for her, if that's what you mean. I care about her.

GIGI. You miss your son.

MARISOL. Yes.

GIGI. I had a brother. He was disabled. He died.

MARISOL. I'm sorry.

GIGI. It was a long time ago. But I get it. They don't get it, but I do.

(Pause.)

Can I smoke in here?

MARISOL. If you want to.

> *(**GIGI** takes out her cigarettes but doesn't light one.)*

GIGI. I was there you know?

MARISOL. Where?

GIGI. The night of the accident.

> *(Small beat.)*

It's okay if you don't want to talk about it.

MARISOL. No, I do. Everyone else likes me to pretend it's not still what I think about most nights. Most days too.

GIGI. Well I was. Anna wants to write me out of it but I have memories too.

MARISOL. Did you go to Princeton?

GIGI. No. We were all just there for the show.

MARISOL. You must have been a baby.

GIGI. I was nineteen.

MARISOL. What do you remember about him?

GIGI. He was drunk. I'm sorry. I think he was on other stuff too. Zach had coke. I remember because I'd never done it before and he gave me some.

MARISOL. Zach?

GIGI. The drummer.

MARISOL. Do you still talk to Zach?

GIGI. No. He lives somewhere. Hawaii, maybe. Or Mexico.

MARISOL. Oh.

GIGI. Well anyway. I don't know what else they were taking but I know that Tommy was drunk and went off by himself and got into a fight with some frat guy.

MARISOL. Yes. I knew that. He had two broken ribs that were unrelated to the accident.

GIGI. I'm probably not going to tell you anything you don't already know.

MARISOL. Just keep going, please.

GIGI. I mean I don't know much because I drove back to the city with Zach.

MARISOL. After he'd been doing drugs?

GIGI. Yeah. It was stupid. But we were fine.

MARISOL. It's crazy isn't it. They drove three miles and you drove two hours and Tommy's the one who…

GIGI. Yeah except.

MARISOL. Except what?

GIGI. We weren't trying to get into an accident.

MARISOL. What do you mean?

GIGI. They were… I'm sorry. I thought you knew this.

MARISOL. I might. I like to hear about it. Call it self-destructive, whatever. I like to relive it.

GIGI. They were trying to hit stuff. Cars and stuff. For fun.

MARISOL. Tommy was.

GIGI. Yeah. I guess he would get in these moods where he wanted to destroy something.

MARISOL. Yes, I know.

GIGI. And I saw him talking to Anna. I don't know what it was about. But he was really upset after. And then they drove home, the three of them, and I think he was just over it. And didn't know how to express it and –

(She stops herself.)

I never talk about this.

MARISOL. You're safe here, honey. No one is going to be mad at you.

GIGI. I was helping Matthew pack up the van. And Anna and Tommy – we couldn't find them so Matthew asked me to go look for them and when I found them they were –
Well.

They were just talking at first but then I think I saw him reach for her. She stopped him and he started screaming at her. Like really screaming. And I don't know. I don't know if that means anything.

She looked really upset but then he just walked away. She was calling after him but he didn't turn around and I guess that's when he went and got in the fight with the frat guy.

When he got back to the van it was weird. The energy was weird. Anna kept trying to make eye contact with him but he wouldn't look at her. She wanted to drive but he wouldn't let her. Matthew told Anna to just get in the car. Then Zach and I left. And I felt sick the whole ride back to the city. I just kept thinking about how he looked like he wanted to hurt them. All of them.

MARISOL. It's okay, we don't have to talk anymore.

>*(Beat.)*

I'm not pretending he didn't have demons. He did. But if you knew him, I mean if you really knew him... He was the sweetest person.

GIGI. I know.

>*(Beat.)*

When do you think they're gonna get back?

MARISOL. I don't know how long these things take.

GIGI. What did you tell her?

MARISOL. That it was a check-up. She's brave. She'll be fine.

GIGI. I think Matthew was more nervous than she was.

MARISOL. If he really wants to do this, he should be able to handle taking her in for the blood work.

GIGI. Oh wow.

MARISOL. What?

GIGI. You're testing him.

MARISOL. No. Not really.

GIGI. It's really nice of you, you know. That you took her in. That you take such good care of her. You're a really good person.

MARISOL. I don't know if that's true. But thank you.

(Beat.)

GIGI. So what are you going to do? After?

MARISOL. After what?

GIGI. The results come back.

MARISOL. Well, it won't be up to me.

GIGI. I think it will. I think you have a say. Matthew wants to fight with Anna. He gets off on it. He won't fight you.

MARISOL. If that's really what this is all about. I'm disappointed. I was hoping they'd grown up more than that.

GIGI. I don't know. Maybe they have. Don't listen to me. No one else does.

MARISOL. No. I'd like to know what you think.

GIGI. I think Matthew would be a good dad.

MARISOL. Is that why you came back?

GIGI. I came back because I don't like the idea of him being on his own.

(Beat.)

And also. I didn't want her to think she still has that much power over me. If I'd left she would have won. I know that's shallow. Now you probably think I'm really immature too.

MARISOL. It doesn't matter what I think.

GIGI. I think it does. I think it matters a lot.

MARISOL. Why?

GIGI. Because everyone wants your approval. They wanted Tommy's approval too – something about your family I guess. Why else would they both have gotten into that car?

MARISOL. It was very foolish.

GIGI. I'm not gonna leave again. If that changes your mind at all. I know I'm no one's idea of responsible – but I'm gonna stay. Just so you know.

MARISOL. Okay.

GIGI. I'm not asking for a chance. I'm not sure I even want it. But whatever happens – I'll stay.

MARISOL. Thanks for letting me know.

GIGI. Sure.

>   *(Beat.)*

I'm not trying to be anyone's mom.

MARISOL. I know.

GIGI. I don't want to replace you. Or Anna.

MARISOL. I don't think that.

GIGI. I feel bad.

MARISOL. For Emma?

GIGI. For all of us, I guess.

MARISOL. Do you want children, Gigi?

GIGI. I don't know.

MARISOL. Thanks for coming.

GIGI. Sure.

MARISOL. It's nice not to be alone.

GIGI. I don't know what I'm supposed to say.

MARISOL. You don't have to say anything, honey. We can just be quiet.

2.6 London

(**ANNA** and **COLIN**, *still in their flat, have been talking for a long time.*)

COLIN. Was he in love with you?

ANNA. No. It wasn't about that. I mean if anything he was in love with Matthew. But it wasn't about that either. Tommy was just. Destructive. And I think maybe I was just the easiest way to ruin everything. I was the fuse that could blow it all up. It's not enviable. It doesn't make you feel good about yourself to realize how disposable you are to the people you love.

COLIN. How do you know she isn't Matthew's?

ANNA. I didn't at first. It was just. Easier if she was Tommy's.

COLIN. Easier?

ANNA. Easier to disconnect. Easier to give her to Marisol. Easier to take the job here, to start over. There was no life for me there. Matthew changed after Tommy. So did I.

COLIN. So you still don't know.

ANNA. No. I know. When I saw her I knew. I knew there was no way she could be Matthew's and that I was making the right choice.

(*Long beat.*)

COLIN. You told me you couldn't.

ANNA. I can't.

COLIN. And you knew, you know how important it is to me. How important it was to my parents.

ANNA. Hasn't it been nice though, just us? Don't we have a nice life?

COLIN. I want a baby, Anna.

ANNA. I know and I'm sorry but I'm never having a child again.

COLIN. Don't I deserve it? For all my suffering? You lied to me, about everything.

ANNA. If I lied to you it was to protect you.

COLIN. From what?

ANNA. You wouldn't have wanted to be with me. If you'd known what I was like then. I'm a horrible person and I hate myself.

COLIN. You knew that life was unsustainable. You were protecting yourself. It's admirable really.

ANNA. You don't believe that. It's selfish. Why are you being nice to me after what I just said to you?

COLIN. I want children, Anna. I still do, with you. This could be a good thing.

ANNA. No, Colin. You don't understand. I wasn't lying when I said I couldn't do it. I'm not capable of being a mother anymore.

COLIN. You think that, but it's not true.

ANNA. It is! I wouldn't love them. That's worse than not having them.

COLIN. How can you say these things? What's the matter with you?

ANNA. This is what I'm trying to tell you. There is a lot that's the matter with me.

COLIN. Anna.

ANNA. I don't understand you. Why aren't you kicking me out right now? Why aren't you screaming?

COLIN. Why would I scream at you?

ANNA. You're not going to change my mind about this. So if you want to leave me, just do it.

COLIN. You don't get out of this that easily.

ANNA. Are you threatening me?

COLIN. No, Anna. I'm married to you. It's not about threats and leaving.

ANNA. Can you try to understand? I need to keep part of myself for her.

COLIN. Children never love the mother who abandoned them.

ANNA. Please don't say that.

COLIN. But with our children. Darling, they'll adore you. Their Mum. Their beautiful Mummy.

ANNA. But I don't want them. I want her.

COLIN. Oh but you will. You'll want ours. You'll see. Once you see them – I know you will.

ANNA. I won't.

>   (**COLIN** *goes to her. Takes her in his arms. Comforts her. She holds on to him.*)

COLIN. Now now, who knows what's best for you? Wittle Anna. Who takes care of you?

ANNA. You do.

COLIN. Who knows how to make you happy?

ANNA. You do.

COLIN. So why don't you trust me? Why don't you ever trust me to know what's best for you.

ANNA. I do trust you.

>   (**COLIN** *holds her.*)

COLIN. I think it's time for Daddy to take care of Mummy. Wouldn't you like that Mummy – to be taken care of?

>   (**ANNA** *puts her head in her hands.*)

Don't cry now. I'm not angry anymore. It was all just a bad dream.

ANNA. Colin.

COLIN. Yes.

ANNA. I'm tired. Will you get me an aspirin?

>   (**COLIN** *goes toward the bathroom.*)

No, they're in my purse.

>   (**COLIN** *takes out Marisol's fancy pillbox. Hands it to* **ANNA.**)

COLIN. What a beautiful box.

>   (*Beat.*)

ANNA. It was my mother's.

COLIN. Shall I run you a bath?

ANNA. No. I need to sleep.

>   *(She starts toward the bedroom.)*

COLIN. Darling.

ANNA. Yes.

COLIN. He could be here by Christmas.

ANNA. Who?

COLIN. Our son.

2.7 New York

(**ANNA**, *very pregnant. Sits at a coffee shop with* **MATTHEW**.)

ANNA. You told Colin.

MATTHEW. You told Gigi.

ANNA. You couldn't even say it to his face.

MATTHEW. A man like Colin. I figured he'd want proof.

(*Small beat.*)

What did he do when he found out?

ANNA. Marked his territory.

MATTHEW. And you obliged?

ANNA. Oh Matthew, didn't you know? I'm such a good little wife.

MATTHEW. Don't be bitter, Anna. Every choice you've made was your own.

ANNA. No. There was one choice I made that wasn't mine.

MATTHEW. What was that?

ANNA. I didn't want to get in the car with Tommy.

MATTHEW. Don't bring this up now.

ANNA. I didn't want to and you forced me.

MATTHEW. Stop.

ANNA. He was too fucked up, he was bleeding and I didn't want to get in the car but you said we'd be home faster if we just gave in and let him drive. You said it was five minutes.

MATTHEW. What would it have changed if you weren't in the car, Anna?

ANNA. It might not have happened.

MATTHEW. Don't make me regret asking you here.

(*Silence.*)

ANNA. I feel like we've died. We're dead.

MATTHEW. Don't be like this. You have a new life now. It's good.

ANNA. Everyone is so goddamn happy for me, it makes me sick. Colin dotes on me, it's disgusting.

MATTHEW. Some women would envy that, you would have envied that. Your nice life.

ANNA. I don't want it anymore.

MATTHEW. Sometimes we're happiest when we stop deciding what we want. God intervenes.

ANNA. Did you just say God?

MATTHEW. Sorry, slipped out.

ANNA. Slipped out of where? You're an atheist.

MATTHEW. Gigi wanted us to go to church, to help deal with all of this.

ANNA. When I think of Gigi I think of cigarettes and spandex. Not crucifixes.

MATTHEW. The two kind of go together don't they? You work in fashion.

ANNA. Don't be funny.

MATTHEW. Having a kid around, Anna. It changes things. You'll see – it's been really – it's nice to think that we're not alone.

ANNA. It's just a phase. Like everything with you.

MATTHEW. No. I don't think so.

ANNA. Next you're going to tell me you stopped drinking.

MATTHEW. I did.

ANNA. Bullshit.

MATTHEW. It's true.

ANNA. For a month, maybe six. I know you.

MATTHEW. You don't know me anymore.

(*Silence.*)

ANNA. How is she?

MATTHEW. She's good. She's adjusting.

ANNA. What does that mean?

MATTHEW. We take her to counseling. She calls it the feelings doctor. Children are malleable, Anna, they adjust.

ANNA. What does she look like?

MATTHEW. She looks like you.

(**ANNA** *wipes a tear from her eye.*)

ANNA. I can't believe Marisol just gave her to you. Just like that. Like she's something she borrowed. I overestimated her.

MATTHEW. She didn't just.

ANNA. What do you mean?

MATTHEW. We had to go through all those tests first. It was intense, and expensive, and hard. There's no "just" in this, Anna. No matter how easy it seems to you from over there.

ANNA. What tests?

MATTHEW. The DNA tests Anna. Jesus.

ANNA. Marisol made you have the test?

MATTHEW. She had to. Because you didn't have the decency to list me as her father.

ANNA. When did this happen?

MATTHEW. Months ago.

ANNA. And?

MATTHEW. What do you mean, and? What do you think, and? Of course, and. And she gave her to me because as you know, I'm her fucking father.

(**COLIN** *enters with shopping bags.*)

COLIN. There she is. My beautiful pregnant wife.

(*He kisses* **ANNA,** *who is in a fog.*)

Hello.

ANNA. Colin, you remember Matthew.

COLIN. Yes. How do you do?

MATTHEW. Congratulations.

(**COLIN** *notices* **ANNA**'s *cup.*)

COLIN. Darling, you really shouldn't be drinking coffee.

ANNA. Please, Colin. It's just one cup.

COLIN. Let me get you a tea. It's better.

(**MATTHEW** *gets up.*)

MATTHEW. I've gotta get going. I'm sure you guys have a lot to do.

COLIN. Yes. Anna's family is in town. We're having a – kind of shower? Don't have those where I'm from. But it's all in good fun.

MATTHEW. Tell your mother I say hello.

COLIN. I think they're thrilled. Never thought this day would come. Took convincing this one.

MATTHEW. I'm happy for you two.

COLIN. And I you. Glad to hear you worked things out with, what was her name, Gigi?

MATTHEW. Yes.

COLIN. Good luck to you both.

MATTHEW. Thanks.

(*Beat.*)

Goodbye, Anna. Be good, okay?

(*He leaves.*)

COLIN. He seems different.

(*He looks at* **ANNA**.)

Are you all right?

(**ANNA** *turns to him.*)

ANNA. She's his.

2.8 Princeton

(Marisol's house is decorated for Christmas.
MATTHEW *is there. He stands next to a large*
tree.)

MATTHEW. Gigi is just finishing a book with her. It's become
their nightly ritual.

MARISOL. That's nice. That they have something.

MATTHEW. I can't thank you enough for letting us come and
spend the night and everything. She was worried Santa
wouldn't find our apartment.

MARISOL. I'm glad you're here. Christmas isn't Christmas
without children.

MATTHEW. We talk about you with her a lot.

MARISOL. That's nice.

MATTHEW. The counselor says it's better. To be very open.
Make it all seem like one big family.

MARISOL. I can understand that.

MATTHEW. Yo creo que nosotros somos familia, Marisol. *[I
think we are family, Marisol.]*

(*Pause.*)

Tommy, Tommy era familia. *[Tommy was family.]*

MARISOL. Okay.

MATTHEW. Sorry.

(*Beat.*)

Ted seems...

MARISOL. Weak as I'm sure you could tell. Pero el sigue.
[But he's surviving.] Though he can't travel anymore.
Which he hates.

MATTHEW. Is it easier? Without Emma?

MARISOL. In some ways it's harder. No distractions. No
ballet class.

MATTHEW. Jesus.

MARISOL. No, I didn't mean that. I just mean – it would be
hard either way.

MATTHEW. It's so unfair. Ted was such a rock.

(**MARISOL** *takes a sip of her drink.*)

You did a good job, Marisol. She's amazing.

MARISOL. Thanks.

MATTHEW. There's something I wanted to ask you.

MARISOL. Sure.

MATTHEW. Emma talks about letters from a pen pal. She wants to know, almost every day, if anything's come for her in the mail. I think it's one of the reasons she was so worried about Santa not knowing where she was. The lack of these letters.

MARISOL. Oh.

MATTHEW. Is it true? Does she have a pen pal? Can you forward her our address?

MARISOL. They're from Anna.

MATTHEW. Anna.

MARISOL. She's been sending them since she was a baby.

MATTHEW. Does Emma know who they're from?

MARISOL. No. It's ambiguous. She just thinks it's her friend.

(*Beat.*)

MATTHEW. What were they like – the letters?

MARISOL. They were nice. Nothing personal. Mostly about things in London, the zoo et cetera... Sometimes they were just little stories. I had always assumed – well, never mind.

MATTHEW. What?

MARISOL. Before things changed I thought that eventually they would be the way in, to an introduction – when she was old enough. Obviously, things are different now. But it seemed clear, at the time, that must have been what Anna thought too.

MATTHEW. Great so now we have to deal with a disappearing pen pal on top of everything else.

MARISOL. I don't think you can blame Anna for this.

MATTHEW. I'm not. It's just another thing you know?

MARISOL. Maybe someday it won't be. Maybe when they're both ready – and you're ready.

MATTHEW. A lo mejor algun dia. Pero no ahora. *[Maybe someday, but not now.]*

MARISOL. No, no ahora. *[No. Not now.]*

(**GIGI** *enters.*)

GIGI. Sorry to interrupt. Emma's asking for her daddy.

MATTHEW. Excuse me.

(*He exits.* **GIGI** *stands with* **MARISOL.**)

GIGI. It's a really nice tree.

MARISOL. Thank you.

(*Beat.*)

GIGI. We've never done a tree. I guess we'll have to start.

MARISOL. Mm.

GIGI. It's pretty.

(*Beat.*)

How do you do it?

MARISOL. What?

GIGI. Put up with all of this shit from everyone.

MARISOL. I don't think of it like that.

GIGI. I'm sorry about your husband.

MARISOL. He's a fighter. Don't worry. We'll be fine.

(*Beat.*)

Can I get you a coquito *[drink]*?

GIGI. No, thank you. I'm, uh – trying not to drink. I don't really drink that much, anyway. Even before. Some nights. Sure. But nothing crazy. I mean, I haven't blacked out in years. But now, with Matthew. I don't want to keep it in the house.

So I dunno, I figure. Why not make it easy. Cut back too. You know?

MARISOL. Sure.

GIGI. I've been buying these seltzers. These like black cherry seltzers. They're okay.

MARISOL. You're a good girl, Gigi.

GIGI. I'm trying really hard.

MARISOL. That's nice.

GIGI. And sometimes it feels like too much. And I just wanna like go on a bender and take a bunch of pills and fuck someone who doesn't love me, you know?

MARISOL. If you were really going to do that, you'd keep it a secret.

GIGI. Anna disappeared. Sometimes I'm at the playground with Emma and I think she could be spying on me.

MARISOL. She didn't disappear. She's at home with her husband and child.

GIGI. I know that. But –

MARISOL. You should feel relieved.

GIGI. I feel like she's waiting in the wings to come and take it all away.

MARISOL. Anna's not malicious, Gigi. She's sad and confused but she's not a mean person.

GIGI. I just wish I knew what she was thinking.

MARISOL. I don't think any of us will ever understand why Anna does the things she does.

GIGI. Thank god for that I guess.

2.9 London

(**ANNA** *is in the kitchen of her and Colin's flat,
also decorated for Christmas. We hear carols
playing softly in the background,* mixed in
with the sound of a baby in the next room.*)

(**ANNA** *stands at the counter with Marisol's
fancy pillbox.*)

(*There's a glass of red wine on the counter.*)

(*She takes the pills out one by one and lines
them up next to the glass of wine.*)

(*She stares at them.*)

(*She swipes them all off the counter and into
her hand. Holds them in her first.*)

(*We hear a key in the lock, and* **COLIN** *enters
with bags of presents.*)

COLIN. Hello darling.

ANNA. Hi. How was your day?

COLIN. Better now that I'm home.

ANNA. Dinner's on.

COLIN. It smells amazing.

ANNA. Thank you.

> (*The baby gives a little whimper from the
> other room.*)

COLIN. Feeding time?

ANNA. Yes.

COLIN. Aren't you going to go in?

ANNA. Could you? I'm a little sore. I pumped earlier.

COLIN. Okay, I'll do it.

ANNA. Thank you.

---

*A license to produce *Nylon* does not include a performance license for
any third-party or copyrighted music. Licensees should create an original
composition or use music in the public domain. For further information,
please see Music Use Note on page 3.

*(**COLIN** picks up a bottle.)*

COLIN. This is ready?

ANNA. Mm-hm.

COLIN. Having some wine?

ANNA. The doctor said it's fine.

COLIN. I know, darling. After Jasper goes down maybe I'll join you for a glass.

ANNA. I'm actually tired. Thinking of having a lie down.

COLIN. All right. When you get up, maybe we can do presents? Just ours before my parents come tomorrow.

ANNA. Sure.

COLIN. Anna.

ANNA. Yes?

COLIN. Can we make a fresh start this year. It's really not as bad as all that, is it?

ANNA. No.

COLIN. Shall I wake you in an hour?

(A whimper.)

ANNA. Colin. The baby.

COLIN. I'm going. Sweet dreams my darling.

ANNA. Good night.

*(**COLIN** takes the bottle and goes into the baby's room; we hear the door shut.)*

*(After a few beats, **ANNA** opens a window and throws the pills out of it before she has a chance to change her mind.)*

*(She's frozen for a moment and then hears **COLIN** cooing the baby in the other room.)*

(She walks to the front door, puts on her shoes and coat, picks up her bag.)

(She grabs the handle. She opens it but then stops herself.)

(She leans against the door. She's exhausted.)

*(In the other room the baby quiets. **COLIN** rocks him, obviously so in love with him.)*

(Whatever has been cooking on the stovetop is starting to burn. Steam rises from the pan.)

*(**ANNA** looks at it. She takes off her coat and hangs it up.)*

(She walks to the stove and picks up a wooden spoon.)

(She stirs the pot.)

(The steam subsides.)

(Silence.)

(Blackout.)

End of Play